AF583408

Original Korean text by Min-ji Jeong
llustrations by Joo-yun Lee

This English edition published by big & SMALL in 2018
by arrangement with Dawoolim
English text edited by Joy Cowley

ISBN: 978-1-925235-31-9
Printed in Korea

See, Hear and Feel!

Written by Min-ji Jeong
Illustrated by Joo-yun Lee
Edited by Joy Cowley

I have two eyes that blink,
a nose with two holes,
two ears that stick out,
a bumpy tongue
and soft skin.

What can I do with them?

I see with my eyes!

I can see everything
when my eyes are open.
I can't see anything
when my eyes are closed.

Your sense of sight depends upon your eyes. But you need light to see. That is why you can see only when your eyes are open.

Animals also **see** with their **eyes**!

An eagle can see long distances with its eyes.

A tarsier's big eyes help it see at night.

A chameleon can move each eye in a different direction.

I smell with my nose!

Your sense of smell depends upon your nose. Smell tells you more about what you see. It helps you taste foods too.

When I smell something good,
I feel good.
When I smell something bad,
I feel bad.

Animals can smell too!

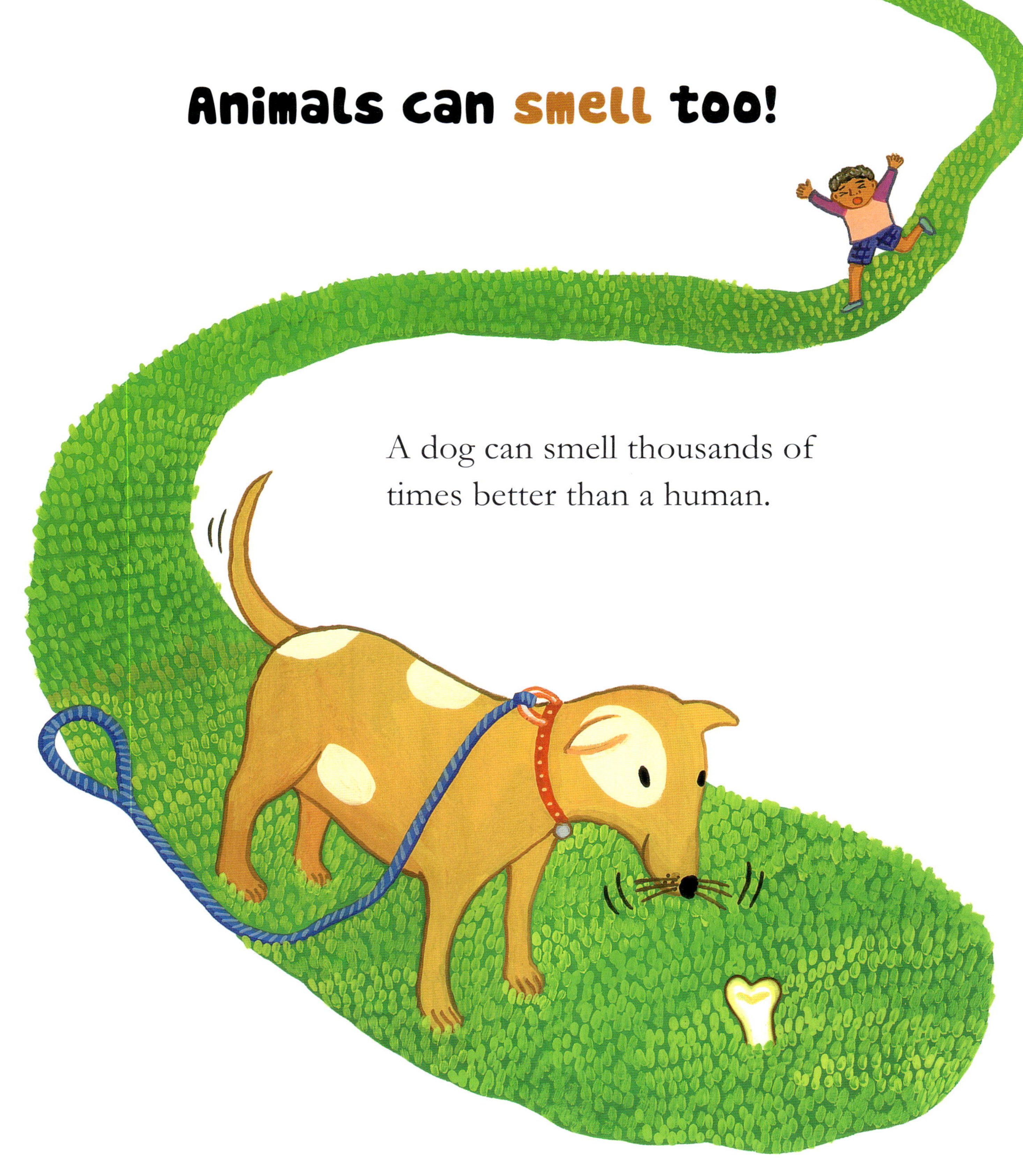

A dog can smell thousands of times better than a human.

A snake can smell
with its flicking tongue.

A shark can smell through
two holes under its snout.

I hear with my ears!

Your ears are organs you use to hear. The ear you see is your outer ear. Inside your head is your inner ear.

A loud sound hurts my ears.

But I want to hear a beautiful sound.

Animals **hear** sounds too!

A grasshopper hears with organs on its belly and front legs.

A dolphin uses its lower jaw to hear friends from far away.

A bat's large ears hear sounds a human cannot hear.

I taste with my tongue!

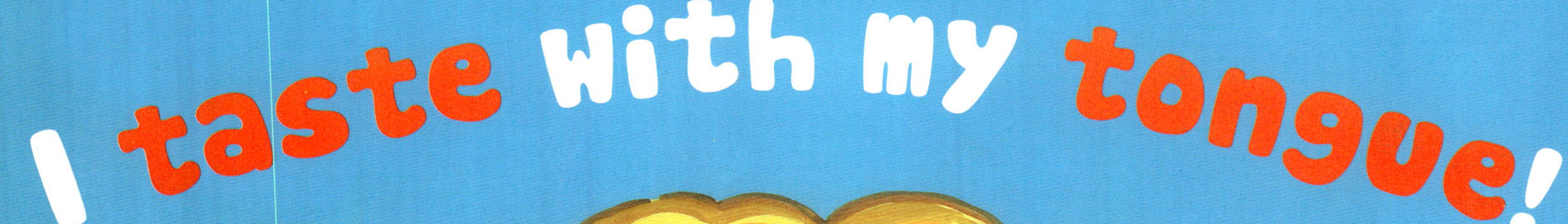

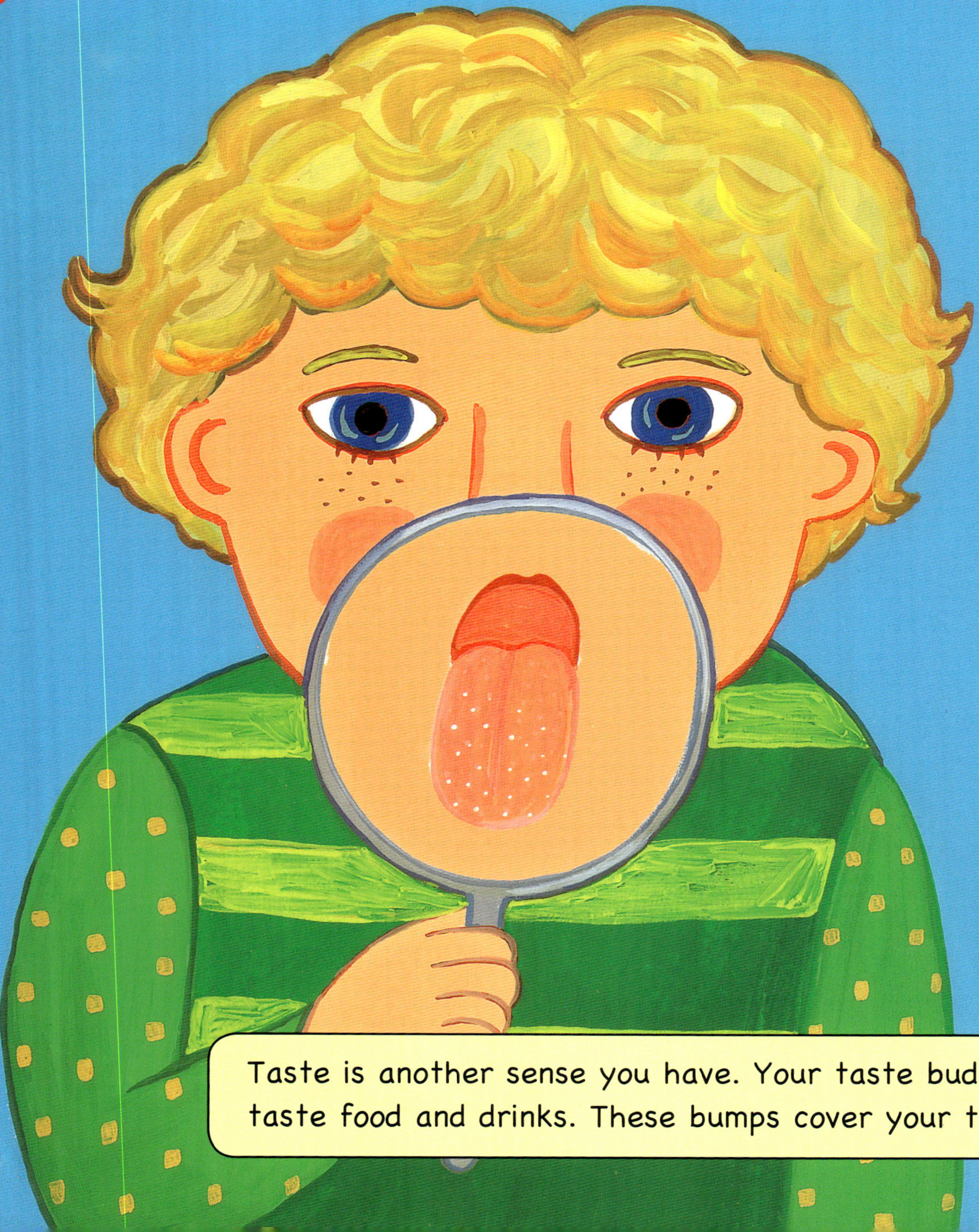

Taste is another sense you have. Your taste buds help you taste food and drinks. These bumps cover your tongue.

I taste sweet, sour and bitter foods
with my tongue.
Candy tastes very sweet.

Animals can also taste!

An ant can taste with its antennae.

A butterfly can taste with its feet.

A carp fish can taste with its lips.

I touch and feel things with my skin!

Touch is another sense. Your skin is your largest organ. It lets you feel things around you.

I touch an ice cube and it feels cold.
It makes my skin tingle.
My mum's face feels warm
and soft against my skin.

Animals **touch** and **feel** things too!

A catfish touches and tastes
with its whiskers.
It tries to find food to eat.

A platypus feels prey
with its bill.

A starfish feels
with the tips of its arms.

We can see, hear, smell, taste and touch many things because we have eyes, ears, a nose, a tongue and skin.

See, Hear and Feel!

Our sense organs send information about the world to our brain. We have five sense organs: our eyes, nose, ears, tongue and skin. These organs help us see, smell, hear, taste and touch. Animals can sense the world too. They use different sense organs. Let's learn about the different ways people and animals sense the world.

Let's think

What happens when our eyes are closed?

How does a snake smell?

Where are a grasshopper's hearing organs?

What does a starfish use to feel things?

Let's do!

Try to guess what objects are without using your eyes! Work in pairs. Blindfold one person. Put some mystery objects in a box. Have the other person pick up an object. Remind the person to use different senses. What does it feel like? What does it smell like? Does it make a sound? Record the person's answers. How many guesses will it take to get the correct answer?